BUMPY RIDE

AN IRON TORNADOES MC ROMANCE
BOOK 7

OLIVIA RIGAL

BUMPY RIDE

AN IRON TORNADOES MC ROMANCE

You'd think I'd know better.

Better than to fall for a biker, and one from a different MC.

Better than to get knocked up by a Nomad who vanished without a trace.

Better than to try and hide it from my family.

This is going to be a bumpy ride.

SPECIAL THANKS TO

Christa Wick
& Zirconia Publishing
who helped me start this Wild Ride.

To find out about her latest release, join her
https://oliviarigal.com/vip-group/

1

DOC

Biker's Heaven is packed tonight. Harleys by the dozens are parked in the small lot next to the bright color neon lights and a few prospects are watching over them.

I spot the kid wearing my colors and park my ride with the other Category 5 Knights bikes. The prospect squints at me; he's a newbie. He's about to protest my parking here when his eyes fall on the Nomad patch. He nods at me and turns his attention to the cute babe who tried to hide behind him as I drove in.

Standards are getting lax, I don't remember being allowed to chat up anyone when I was a prospect on guard duty. But then again my president was Stallion and he was a mean son of a bitch. Can't say I felt bad when I learned he'd been murdered by the asshole supremacists he had associated the club with. My home chapter closing was sad though.

Entering the bar, I scan the room. It's hard to see through the smoke, but I spot a handful of Knights sitting together and make my way to their table. There're a couple of locals I know, some I don't, and another Nomad I've shared bits of roads with.

Prince is an interesting guy, not a talker. He was the sergeant-at-arms of the South Florida chapter when the shit hit the fan. "It was rough, man ... but then Stallion got what was coming to him." It's the only thing he ever said when I asked him about it, and it's the longest statement I've ever heard him make. This one beat his previous record by three words, if I have my counts correct.

As soon as I get my butt on a chair, a waitress comes with fresh drinks. She's a skinny sort of girl, so tiny I half expect her to topple under the weight of her loaded tray. The twig notices me and comes closer, "Hey handsome," she purrs, "what can I get you?"

I smile at her attempt at seduction. Not my type at all. I like a woman with a lot more curves.

"I'll have a draft and a Bunny," I tell her.

She frowns. "A Bunny?"

Prince and the other guys laugh. She has no clue what I'm talking about.

One of the guy grabs her by the waist and says, "Don't you wrinkle your pretty nose. You're Bunny's replacement, sweetheart."

"Oh, that Bunny," she says as the light bulb flashes on in her mind. "Yeah, got it. Her name is still on my locker door."

"When did she leave?" My frustration is such that I bark the question at the poor girl who takes one step back.

"I don't know, Doc. End of August, I'd say." The local Prez scratches his head and then nods, "Yeah, that's right. It was 'bout a couple weeks ago. The time my kid started college. Bunny gave my daughter all her stuff before she left. So yeah, end of August."

Fuck. I'm too late. When I left in June, I'd asked her to wait and told her I'd be back soon. I didn't expect to be away so long. I should have called, but every day one thing led to another and I couldn't get free before the Labor Day weekend.

Did she wait? Maybe, maybe not. Maybe she did and then gave up on me. In her shoes, I would have thought I wasn't coming back. Either way, it sucks.

Who's stupid enough to ride across three states for a woman without checking she'll be around when he arrives? Me, that's who. But then, the past months have been so damned hard, the only thing I could do at the end of my shifts was collapse into bed. I probably haven't had a coherent non-medical thought in weeks.

And now she's gone. Fuck me sideways. I need a place to crash tonight before I ride back tomorrow. I'm frustrated. A good old fashion bar fight would be perfect to let off some steam, but it's probably not a good idea. The last thing I need right now is to get arrested or injure my hands.

I don't need to give the chief of surgery an excuse to fuck with me. He's already resentful enough that my army connections forced the hospital to accept me in his program. I don't need to aggravate him more.

"Come on," Prince says after the waitress returns with my drink. "Looks like you need a change of pace. There's a pool table with my quarters on it."

I follow him to the adjacent room which houses a dozen pool tables, two of which are available. The chick in charge of running the place greets him with a big smile.

"Hello, my Prince," she says. "Your table is waiting and I kept your favorite one for you."

"Thank you, babe," he answers giving her a brotherly hug.

He sighs as he watches her walk away exaggerating the swing of her hips. "If she wasn't Sam's daughter..."

He doesn't need to finish his sentence. That temptress is forbidden territory to all patrons of Biker's Heaven. Sam runs his bar with an iron fist. He's made sure everyone knows his little girl is off limits. But she's twenty, sizzling hot, and provocative as fuck. Some day one guy's gonna flip, and he'll have hell to pay.

Prince grins as he looks away. It's the first time I've seen him so laid back and talkative.

"Did you decide what you were gonna do after your residency?" he asks.

I shake my head. I've given up on making long terms plans. Every time I do, they backfire on me. I'm just gonna go with the flow. My only plan is to lay on a beach somewhere for a full week after I'm done with this final term at the hospital from hell.

"'Cause I know just the place where you could fit in." He pauses to put the blue chalk away and place the cue ball. I wait for him to tell me more, looking at the rack of sticks. Pool is not my game, and I have no idea how to tell which stick would be the best suited for me.

"I'm moving back to South Florida," he says, breaking with a solid shot that spreads the balls around and sinks the eleven and the twelve. "Looks like I'm stripes, this round. A new chapter opened in the spring in Defiance and I'm going to be their Sergeant-at-Arms. It's a young crew and they're looking for new blood."

I nod and play with the idea in my head.

Still smiling, Prince continues, "And you know, a doctor is always a welcomed addition to a club."

Defiance is a few miles from where our old chapter was. If I remember correctly, there are a few hospitals in the area. Might be worth a shot to apply at the VA hospital. I could be useful there. They're always damn understaffed, might be a sure thing. Also, I'd be closer to my grandmother who's not getting any younger.

"And there's something else. Let's call it a signing bonus." Prince looks up from the table at me with a malicious grin. *He's dangling a worm in front of me. I can see the hook right there, shiny and barbed. But that worm's just so tasty. Fuck it.* "Yeah? What would that be?" *Chomp.*

"For such a smart guy, Doc, you're a *dumbass* sometimes. Where's Bunny from? Where'd she grow up?"

"Point Lookout. But, look, how do I know she moved back home when she finished her degree? She could have gone anywhere."

"Right, right. How *could* you know? Maybe you could ask someone who rides through there every couple weeks." In the smoky light, Prince's grin looks positively satanic. "If only you knew *someone* who does that."

No way. No fucking way. How had I not thought of this before? The last tiny ember of uncrushed hope in me glows, flickers, as fresh oxygen and fuel trickle in.

"Don't fuck with me, brother." My warning is soft, but it's deadly serious. Prince spreads his hands and shrugs. He still has that grin. *Sign here, please. All your dreams will come true, and what do you need that soul for anyway?* "Is she there or not?"

"Yeah, Doc. She's there." His smile grows as he watches my expression change. So much for keeping a poker face.

"How do you know?"

"How the hell do you think? I *saw* her there when I went through there last," he answers. "She's working with her sister in the town hotel."

Figures. Her degree is in hospitality.

I hang around a while watching Prince play. He's got a point. South Florida is home.

And then there's Bunny ...

2

BUNNY

I promised myself I wouldn't, but I can't help myself. I dial Biker's Heaven. A few rings and someone picks up. The first thing I hear is the familiar background hum of the bar and then a voice.

"Yeah, what?" Sam's greeting is always the same. It cracks me up. He's the living proof that constant courtesy is not as indispensable as I was taught in college for success in our line of business.

"It's nice to hear your voice too," I tell him. Despite his bark, I'm not sarcastic. Working with him was easier than working with the stuffed shirts of Point Lookout Central Hotel.

They're all about rules and protocols that don't make much sense. Sam didn't set absurd rules. He didn't care how you organized yourself. As long as you got things done and the patrons were happy, he was happy.

"Hey, Bunny, sweetheart, how are you?" All aggression vanishes from his voice. "How's Florida treating you?"

"It's good. I mean, I miss you, of course, but I'm doing well. Working for you was more fun that what I'm doing now," I confess. "But you know, there's the family and all that. It's nice to be back home with them. I missed my sisters."

Sam laughs. "Is it true what I heard? Brains finally managed to produce a son?"

"Yes, he did!" We chat for a while about my dad's latest old lady and the baby boy they're so proud of. Not that he doesn't love us to bits, but let's face it, after six daughters, the man deserved a break.

Mimi, my Haitian friend suggested to call him Désiré which means *wanted* in Créole or French. It's a traditional name in Haiti for a kid who took a long time to come, but Dad went for Jack instead. Nice and simple.

"I guess you didn't call just to check up on me," Sam says when we're done talking about my family. The man's sharp, he know why I'm nervous and talking a mile a minute. "Well, I'm sorry, honey, but your Knight came in a few weeks ago when I was out. I couldn't give him your note."

"Oh!" I try to hide the disappointment from my tone, but there's a ball in my throat that prevents me from saying anything else.

"Do you want me to give it to another Knight?" he asks.

I take a deep breath and find my voice, "No, it's good. Trash it."

"Fine, I will. Okay, kiddo, work calls. I gotta go. Later, gator!"

"Thanks, for everything..." He hangs up before I could finish my sentence. It's just as well, he doesn't like mushy and neither do I.

I drag myself away from my table to my rocking chair. It's old, battered and ugly, but I love it. My ma, sisters, and I were rocked to sleep in it. I put my hands on my tummy. There's not much of a visible bump because I was round to begin with.

Yet I know someone's there, slowly growing in me and I smile thinking my baby will be the next one to fall asleep in that chair.

A knock on the door startles me. Guess I catnapped. Before I make my way to the door, Everest enters carrying what looks like half a dozen pizza boxes and a large bag.

"Dinner is served," my handsome friend announces as he walks by me and sets the pizzas on my table. He makes quick work of putting in one pile all the papers scattered around. "You need a desk," he notes.

"That, a cradle, and a life," I answer.

"Well, life is coming."

I follow him into the kitchen where he pulls out from his bag an assortment of paper plates, plastic cups, napkins, and fresh beers. "You're having a crowd tonight. Lisa and Ice as well as Mimi and David."

Mentally, I go through every room in the house trying to figure out if I have enough chairs when Everest says, "Your grandma had folding chairs in the garden shed. I'll get them."

The man has an extraordinary memory. Now that he mentions it, I recall we used to get patio chairs from the backyard when Grandma had those large barbecues where we could bring along anyone. Her shed is folding chair central. Everest remembers; he never missed any of those parties. His brother Ice also tagged along the summers.

What I want for my kid is a childhood as happy as mine was. Not that it was perfect, but all things considered, it was good. Yep, that's the best thing I can give him or her.

Everest is out and back in a dash. As he helps me wipe them clean of the cobwebs, he asks, "Any news?"

After a second of hesitation, I shake my head. Before I have a chance to tell him of my conversation with Sam, the door opens to Birdy and Kitty.

"We saw Everest arriving with the pizzas and decided it would be more fun having dinner here than at home," Birdy says.

"But we didn't come empty handed." Kitty pulls her hands from behind her back and shows triumphantly two giant containers of ice cream. She looks delighted with herself.

Everest winks at me. I know what he's thinking. How easy and carefree our lives were when we were their age. We didn't have a care in the world. Well, we did, but in hindsight we realize they were childish worries.

Now I worry that my two sisters have left my mother alone after she's prepared dinner for them. She's a horrible cook but still, that wouldn't be nice.

A glance through the kitchen windows reassures me. Only Birdy's car is parked in front of my mother's house. Since those two were left to fend for themselves, they were right to come over.

While Kitty puts her two containers in the freezer, Birdy looks around the living room and opens the two bedroom doors. The smaller room still houses the bunk beds we slept in when we had sleep over at Granny's house, the other hasn't changed much. I just got a new bed.

"You've been here for weeks and you haven't changed anything, have you?" she asks, not noticing my new king-size playground.

"Not for now," I admit. "I'll save up and redo one room at a time."

"And ours will be the baby's room?" Birdy asks.

I stare at her dumbfounded. I didn't tell my family yet. How does she know?

"Oh come on, don't look surprised," Kitty adds. "We can hear you puking every morning and you've been looking all weird. You know, thoughtful and shit." Kitty sure has a way with words.

"Yeah, everyone figured it out. What do you think, that we're all blind and dumb?" says Lisa as she and Ice walk through the kitchen door which Everest left open as he brought chairs in.

"The only thing we don't know is who the father is," Mimi chimes in holding the door for David holding a huge box from the Cheesecake Factory. Mimi knows I have a passion for their Godiva chocolate cake. I wonder how it will taste with a ball of Kitty's vanilla ice cream.

David frowns at Mimi's question, but no one notices. He and Everest are the only ones of the group who have some sort of grasp on the concept of privacy.

"She'll tell you when she's good and ready," Everest snaps back curtly as he opens the pizza boxes on the large table. He then turns to Mimi and gives her his best smile. Typical Everest attitude. A perfect mixture of rough and sweet. "Come on, guys, dig in while it's still warm."

Everest knows, but will never tell. I can trust him. All my secrets are safe with him.

As we take our seats around the table, I wonder what my grandma would say if she could see us. I'm sure she'd be happy to see I'm living in the house she left me. And I'm delighted to have it, even if it's a bit too close to my mom's place. What she would worry about is how I'm going to raise a child on my own. I worry about that too. I so want to be a great mom.

"Did you hear Prince was back?" Mimi asks to no one in particular.

"I knew a Knight with that name," I answer.

"Tall, dark, and handsome?" Ice frowns at Lisa's question. "What?" she protests. "I can think a man is handsome without any afterthought." She acts offended, but I know she likes when Ice acts jealous.

"Yep, very dark. Did he join the Defiance chapter?" I ask.

Ice answers. "Yes, he's back and he's their Sergeant-at-Arms again." He takes a deep breath and his gaze gets lost in the distance.

I'm suddenly connecting the dots. I'd heard that Juliya--Ice and Everest's sister--had fallen head over heels for the member of another MC called Prince. This is interesting. There can't be that many Princes among the Knights. This may be why Everest looks preoccupied.

According to Lisa and Mimi, who can be chatty some days, when Juliya and Prince were in the same room, there was enough electricity in the air to feed a small city.

Everest mentioned in passing that he was happy the guy was gone. For him, the problem was not so much that Prince was from another MC. He said he could work with that if it made his sister happy.

The problem was that even Whiz, the Tornado intel expert, was unable to get anything on the man. And if there's one thing Everest and Ice don't like it's a nut they can't crack.

"Good thing all your disputes ended with Stallion. You get along fine with the new team, right?" Lisa comments. "Also, Juliya has done a few favors for their VP so they owe you now."

"Yeah, they're mainly good people," Ice agrees a bit grumpily. "Chaser told me they were expecting a new interesting addition."

"Yeah, what kind?" Everest asks.

"A doc. The guy's about our age, maybe a little older. He's ex-military, like me and David ..."

My heart is racing and blood is pounding in my ears like a jungle drum. I don't hear the rest of Ice's answer. I can't hear a thing anymore. Everest notices and squeezes my hand under the table. His warmth soothes me and I stop fighting my feelings ... I'm letting hope in.

I'm a sucker for stories with a happy ending so--just for a moment--I'm going to allow myself to dream.

I'll dream it's no coincidence, and he's decided to come here. I'll dream he followed me here.

I'll dream the coming year will be happy.

I'll dream ... because I've always been a dreamer.

3

DOC

I wanted to stop at Biker's Heaven on my way south and hang out with the local chapter for a few days, but I changed my mind when I saw the weather forecast. Another cold front is coming. It will hit full blast on Christmas day. I want to get to Florida before the roads are covered with black ice.

After Chaser, the Prez for South Florida, made it official, it took me a month to answer Prince's proposal to join the Defiance Chapter. I told them I needed time to think about it, but the truth is, I decided to go the very second I was told about the creation of the chapter.

It's good to go back home.

The last part of the ride feels the longest, but I finally make it to the compound.

Last spring, the MC purchased an abandoned farm and all the available acres of land around. I'm impressed with what they've done with it in such a short time.

In addition to the clubhouse, there's a cluster of small buildings. The color of the painted wood makes it easy to tell the new construction from the older, but nothing sticks out like a sore thumb.

What was a barn at some point is now a workshop for bikes and next to it there's a playground complete with swings and monkey bars.

I guess the members of this new chapter must be around my age and starting families. That should be interesting.

There's not a kid in sight, though.

When I first joined, kids were only allowed on the MC grounds when we had special family events. The rest of the time, there were way too many Sweet butts roaming around for any of the patched members to consider having their family around. It would have killed the permanent party mood.

Maybe this new style is best, especially to keep a low profile with the rest of the community. Yeah, family life is the best cover ever. Color me cynical, but I have no illusions. There's no way the activities of this club are 100 percent legit.

Prince's already told me they run meds in the country. They're being smart about it; they run prescription stuff that cannot be used for recreational purposes. I looked at the list of what they import, and I don't know who came up with it, but it's good.

They drive in meds most senior citizens need and sell them cheap. All that stuff can be purchased for a fraction of the price in Canada or South America.

I wonder what else they do that made them so excited about my joining them. I'll find out soon enough for sure.

At the sound of my arrival, a prospect comes out from the clubhouse. He greets me and shows me where to park my ride.

"Wanna see your crib first or join the others in the main room?" he asks.

"Crib first," I tell him and he guides me to one of the older structures.

"You scored Piston's place," he tells me leading me into a very large bedroom.

"Why is that?" I ask, opening a door to a decent size bathroom. There's a tiny sink, a toilet, and a shower large enough to accommodate three people at the same time. It's not luxurious, but much better than what I expected.

"His old lady came equipped with a kid so, you know, they needed a larger place." He shrugs and turns to leave. "Whenever you're ready, we're all in the main room of the clubhouse."

"Thanks, I'll be there in a bit."

He steps out, and as he closes the door behind him, I realize I didn't even ask for a name.

I throw my saddle bags by the side of the bed and decide to unpack later. There's not much to put away. I'm light on clothes since the bulk of my luggage is my emergency kit. I can't be bothered to unpack now; I'm famished.

While washing my hands, I look at myself in the mirror and consider shaving. Nah, I'll do it when I'll start working. I look like death warmed over. I spent the past six months working like a madman without showing my face to the sun. I badly need some rest. Sleep is what this doctor prescribes.

There's a key on my door, but I ignore it and walk out without bothering to lock it. I can't think of anywhere safer for my stuff. I retrace my steps to the clubhouse.

The first floor of the reconverted farmhouse boasts two banquet-size tables complete with benches. I count twenty brothers settled around the largest table with an assortments of chicks who all look yummy enough to be Sweet butts, but could just as well be old ladies. Half a dozen kids sit at the other table, under the supervision of another handful of girls.

No property patch on any of the woman. I'm not certain how much I like this new organization. How the fuck does one tell who's who?

Prince sees me and waves from the other side of the room. As I come closer, his powerful voice carries over everyone else's and breaks the chatter. "Guys, meet Doc!" A chorus of voices answers. I catch a few names in the ruckus.

There's Chaser at the end of the table. On his left, a sexy brunette and on his right, his VP, Piston's holding a blond bombshell on his lap. They both nod.

Across from Prince, there's Dragon. The name will be easy to remember. The man has an impressive Chinese style tattoo. A colorful beast is etched on his arm. Next to him, there's a sort of giant called Peanut. I wonder if it's the size of his nuts or the size of his brains that earned him that name.

He smiles in earnest shaking his head up and down like a toy. I'm tempted to think he is what my grandma calls a pure-heart. It's her southern polite way to designate someone who's not all there.

"Raven, give Doc your seat and get your ass to the other table," another guy barks.

A young girl stands. "Yes, sir," she grumbles, and though she obeys, it's clear she's not happy to be relegated to the kid's table.

I look at her and wonder if she's jail bait. If she's not, she's barely passed eighteen. She's emaciated and about as pale as I am. No one should be that pale in Florida. Despite the dark make up she hides behind, her face is sort of pretty.

The conversations restart as I take her seat. Before she moves away, I catch her arm and say, "Thank you."

She shrugs and looks at my hand on her arms as if it were a venomous spider. I let her go and she mumbles, "Thanks for nothing."

I'm now sitting next to Peanut who's probably not as dim witted as I imagine cause he reads the question in my eyes and explains, "Raven is Thor's daughter." With a movement of his chin, he designates the man who asked her to move to the other table.

"Thanks," I say and he smiles again.

"So, Doc," he asks, "is it true you're a real doc?"

As I nod, about to tell him more, he changes the subject. "Do you like fireworks, Doc? 'Cause on New Year's Eve there's a big fireworks show on the beach at Point Lookout and we're all going. I love fireworks, don't you?"

I don't need to answer him. He's happy rambling on about all the fireworks he's seen, and of course, his favorite was in Orlando ...

Prince rolls his eyes and sighs as he passes me a plate with turkey and sweet potato fries. Some of the brothers look exasperated by Peanut's endless flow, but yet no one tries to make him shut up. They seem to have made their peace with the fact he's the mandatory simple cousin, the one special relative without which no family is complete.

Somehow it gives the dinner a homey feeling.

That sort of brotherhood is why I joined the MC to begin with. I needed a shelter and they provided one.

The Category 5 Knights are my family.

It's good to be home.

4

BUNNY

From my office at the Central Hotel, I overlook A1A. I go through the motions while glancing out the window every time I hear the distinctive sound of a Harley engine. There's a lot of those today. Everyone is riding into town for the fireworks.

"What's so interesting outside?" my boss asks, catching me looking out the window again.

"The crowd you've drawn," I answer sweetly. "I'm really impressed by how well this special event is organized. I mean it's the only thing everyone has been talking about all week."

The little man literally puffs up with pride. He's the second-in-command of the place and should be overseeing the day to day operations. He doesn't. Instead leaves most of it to my sole discretion.

Daily routine is boring for him. He doesn't want to take care of business, yet he can't be bothered to look past the set of rules he'd given me on the day I started. Anytime I suggest revisiting them, his eyes glaze over.

Rumor has it the only thing he cares about is organizing large events. I heard the 4th of July party he put together this summer was wild, and he always manages to find something to outshine the previous event.

He comes and stands next to me by the window. "I guess I'd better go double check that everything is ready," he says.

"Great idea," I concur. Anything to get him out of my hair. Everest and the rest of the gang are picking me up in a bit. I need to finish sorting the billing mess on my desk.

The restaurant's manager was just let go after the top brass figured out he was keeping a separate set of books, hence depriving the hotel of its cut on the profits.

Just as I'm about to return to my desk, I return to the window. Yes, that was an Harley engine roar. The Knights ride in. There's about twenty, and I scan their bikes looking for Doc's ride. My heart skips a bit as I recognize him in the pack.

My spirit soars as I imagine our reunion. I've played this scene about a thousand times in my mind. He sees me, smiles and opens his arms. I run to him and ...

Fuck, fuck, fuck! There's a girl behind him.

Okay, Bunny, let's not get carried away. Deep breath. Just because she's riding with him doesn't mean she's with him. I force myself to take another deep breath. Right, everyone's coming to see the fireworks and there's nothing more natural than to give a ride to some of the girls of the community.

Even if she's a Sweet-butt.

Right. I need to convince myself it doesn't mean a thing.

I watch the girl get down from the bike. She's tall, almost as tall as he is. She's young, thin, too, and when she removes her helmet, magnificent jet black hair cascades around her face. I hate her instantly, and when I see the way she adoringly looks up at Doc I want to claw her eyes out.

The skinny girl says something and Doc turns around. He pauses for a second and laughs. He throws his head back as if what she's just said is the funniest thing ever. She blushes like a teenager. Her smile grows huge, she's clearly delighted she's amused him.

He says something back and ruffles her hair. Good. That's a gesture a man has for a kid, not for a woman. She playfully punches his arm. Yep, they behave like siblings ... until he picks her up cave man style and then I wonder. I watch them walk away from my line of vision, him laughing and her pounding ineffectively against his back.

Ugly, jealousy tears my heart open, and for a moment I forget to breathe. Yet, somehow I find my way back to my desk and attempt to fight the green monster. I fail miserably. I look at the paperwork on my desk, but all I can see is him walking away, carrying her on his shoulder.

I take a deep breath. Again.

She *is* his, she must be.

Deep breath, and another.

I'm not upset; fine, not *that* upset.

I shouldn't be upset.

Okay, I'm crying but it's the hormones.

Everyone knows pregnant women are hormonal.

Gosh, I need to concentrate. I must not think about what I just saw. For all I know, she could be his kid sister. Except he told me he was a single child. But she still could be a younger cousin. Right, he never said he didn't have cousins.

Out of sheer will, I manage to focus on my work for the remaining hour of my workday. The numbers on the sheet are a nice way to escape reality. Numbers are my friends, numbers are easy, they add up or they don't. Numbers don't cheat, numbers don't lie ... well not under close scrutiny.

When I'm done I run to the bathroom and wipe my face. The woman staring back at me in the mirror has puffy eyes and looks like she needs sleep. I close my eyes and the image of Doc's girl appears in my head. She's everything I'm not, tall, thin and elegant. She's like a young and delicate feline and I ... well, I feel like a whale washed ashore.

Before I come out with other unflattering images for myself, Birdy enters the ladies' room.

"There you are," she says. "I was looking all over for you." Looking at my face she raises an inquisitive eyebrow. I shake my head.

"Give me a minute. I'm almost ready."

She follows me to my office to get my bag.

"Were you throwing up again?" she asks. "I thought that was supposed to stop after the first trimester."

I shrug in a noncommittal fashion. I'm happy she thinks my eyes were wet because I had been sick. I don't feel like answering any questions.

After packing my bag, I lock my office door and force a smile on my face. As we walk by the huge lobby bar of the hotel, Birdy waves to the other bartenders. One of them was more than happy to swap shift with her. New Year's Eve tips are usually very good and unlike my sister, the girl has bills to pay.

As far as Birdy's concerned, her salary is pocket money. She's got room and board for free at Mom's house, so she can spend her money on herself.

Once I asked her if she was setting money aside and she looked at me as if I had two heads. She didn't answer, so I have no clue what her expression meant. Hopefully she knows it's good to have something for a rainy day, but somehow I doubt it. She'll live and learn ... or she'll ask our father. I wonder how he's doing these days. One thing for sure, his new wife doesn't seem to lack for anything.

Everest is waiting for us at the bottom of the hotel steps and he takes my arm to help me cross the street. I laugh, and even though I protest out of principle at his overprotecting me, I'm happy he's here.

We reach the beach and see hands rise and wave at us guiding us to a patch of sand that has been claimed by the Tornadoes. Coolers with drinks and ice litter the beach, and a mini stereo perched precariously on top of one blasts Blue Oyster Cult ...In our extended family hard rock still rules.

I sit next to Mimi and try to make myself comfortable while Everest gets us drinks. A bottle of water for Mimi and me. I look curiously at Mimi who usually drinks beer but do not comment.

I throw a look at her belly, but she's like me, a very curvy girl so it may be too early for anything to show if what I suspect is true.

Toussaint, her nephew and adopted son, comes to say hello and then rushes away to hang out with the younger crowd. Mimi sighs, "Ah, to be young again."

Just as I struggle finding a good position sitting up, Everest comes and sits behind me. He spreads his legs and pulls me up ordering me to use him as a back rest. I lean against him, thankful for the comfort he gives me.

"So what happened?" he whispers in my ears while Mimi looks away keeping an eye on her son.

"What do you mean?" My attempt to play dumb doesn't fly. I can't see Everest's face, but I hear him growl softly so I relent. "I saw him," I confess.

"And?"

"He's with another girl." I keep my answers short. No need to explain, I'm sure he understands, and furthermore, if I start talking about the way I feel, I'm going to cry... again.

Of course, I could always blame my tears on my *condition*. That's the perfect excuse, especially for me since I've always been moody. Yet, I'd rather focus on something else and enjoy the company of my friends. Tonight, when I'm alone in my bed, it will be time enough to sob miserably.

The baby kicks and I invite Everest to lay his hands flat on my belly to see what his future godchild is doing. He rests his palms and chuckles softly.

"It's the ocean. The kid hears the waves and want to go surfing."

I rest my head against his broad chest and sigh. I'm so grateful he's there for me. I hope one day I can repay him.

5

DOC

A good deed never goes unpunished. I never should have been nice to Raven; she's sticking to me like gum on the sole of my boot. Kid's so attention starved, it's like kicking a puppy to push her away.

Unlike Peanut, my other newly adopted friend, I don't really care for fireworks. The only reason I'm here is to take advantage of this big gathering to reach out to the Iron Tornadoes.

Now I've rested enough. All my ducks are in a row... ready to work at my command. It's finally time to find Bunny... figure out what she's doing. I want, even need her back. The craving I have for this woman is so fucking weird. It's like no one else can spark any interest. The club's Sweet butts have tried their best, but now they've about given up on me.

The only one who's still trying is Raven.

Because I've gone soft? Fuck me, I've gone way beyond the call of duty by treating her to a light dinner in one of the specialty booth set up by the beach for the evening. I shouldn't have. Now no matter what I say, I can't seem to shake her loose.

"Why don't you go join the rest of the crowd?" I ask pointing in the direction of the spot on the beach where the Knights have set camp.

Raven shakes her head and gives me her best smile.

"I'm having fun with you," she says batting her lashes. "I'm happy to stick around whatever you wanna do."

I resist the impulse to roll my eyes at her. Even though she's nineteen, when I look at her I see a child and I'm no cradle robber. My taste goes to women. Round, luscious, grown up. Not kids. She's cute, but no.

On the other hand, I noticed one of the prospects is sweet on her. He looks at her with adoring eyes, but so far he hasn't made a move. Poor guy is terrified by her father. Can't say I blame him, even I find Thor a bit intimidating.

The man's not running for father of the year title. He's as indifferent to the twin boys his new Old Lady popped out that he is to Raven.

From the road, I scan the crowd looking for an Iron Tornadoes patch, but I can't see a thing. I leave the asphalt to walk on the beach and Raven catches my arm. She leans against me more than necessary to remove her heels and follows me dutifully like an obedient puppy.

I give up for now and lead her back to the fold. Most of the members of the MC have set up camp on the beach. The younger kids are running around in the sand, delighted with the opportunity to keep on playing past their bed times. It's chilly, well, by Florida standards at least, and we're all bundled up.

"What would be nice would be a campfire," I say to no one in particular as I reach for one beer from the cooler. I hesitate, normally I'd take two and give one to Raven, but she's like a stray. If I want her to go away, I've got to stop feeding her.

"Fires aren't allowed on the beach," Raven says.

"So? Didn't stop the Tornadoes from building one," Belle notes looking from us to another side of the beach.

Piston laughs and says, "It sure helps having a cop as a member of your team." He points to a very tall guy who's standing next to a raging fire. "See that guy? That's Everest, he's their Prez's brother. And a cop;

works for the Point Lookout Force. One foot on each side of the fence."

I observe the giant as pulls a woman to her feet. She come closer to the flames. He rubs her shoulder as she leans against him. Fuck that's *my* Bunny!

"Oh, how sweet," Belle says. "Everest and Bunny are back together!"

My teeth clench as I squint at the couple.

What is she doing leaning into that man.

Without turning to look at Belle, I ask, "Bunny?"

"Bunny's the eldest of the Ryan girls," she explains. "She's MC royalty, so to speak. I know her cause we grew up together in Point Lookout. I went to school with her and Birdy. They have a younger sister called Kitty and then another bunch of sisters but much younger, by a different mom."

I ask, "So, Bunny and Everest?" It's all the prompt Belle needs to go on.

She shakes her blond mane and continues, "Yeah, those two were an item all through high school. I thought they had called it off when Everest left for college. I remember a few years back he was engaged to a girl from Miami. Guess that didn't work out."

Belle's a happy soul and probably doesn't think of relaying this information as gossip.

Sitting next to her, Holly says, "The furthest I've ever driven is Orlando. Some days I wish I could have gone to college and visited other parts of the country, but most of the time I figure, I have all I need in Defiance."

Her wistful tone catches Chaser attention and reels him in like a hooked fish. He crouches before her and grabs a fistful of her hair. He tilts her head and looks at her hungrily.

"You better believe it, sweetheart. All you'll ever need is right here."

As he bends over to kiss her, the kids around us make gagging noise. The scene is too mushy for them. I turn back in the direction of the fire. And all I see now are silhouettes against the light of the flames.

I resist the urge to walk over and claim my girl. I know better. This is not the right time, not the right place.

I hate to admit it but I need to figure this out ... We're at peace with the Tornadoes. Chaser and Piston have a few deals going with them. I'm too new to the chapter to jeopardize the situation of the club over a piece of ass no matter how juicy it is.

I grind my teeth. Who am I kidding? Bunny's more than just a piece of ass.

Making a mental note to question Belle to get more intel on Bunny, I finish my beer and settle on the sand to watch the fireworks. Raven comes to me with another bottle and finds a spot very close to me. She shivers a bit and without thinking, I put an arm around her shoulders.

When she leans against me for warmth, I make two New Year's resolution.

First, and foremost, get my girl.

Second, stop feeding the strays.

6

BUNNY

The beach turns dark and the only spots of light, aside from the street lampposts on the road, is the campfire we have built. I lean against Everest who pulled a cozy blanket from his saddle bag and wrapped it around me.

Ice and Lisa arrive just before the show begins.

"Where were you?" Everest asks his brother.

"Visiting the Knights," Lisa answers for him. She's been doing that a lot lately, the answering for him, and surprisingly it doesn't seem to get on his nerves as I suspected it would.

"Yeah, we've got a few projects with them," Ice adds.

Everest raises a questioning eyebrow and Ice shrugs away his silent interrogations, "You don't wanna know, Officer Hatcher."

"If you say so, Prez," Everest answers with good humor.

"We met one of their new members," Lisa says.

"Oh yeah?" I already know what's coming and I want to punch Everest for fishing for information.

"Yeah, his name is Doc and he's a real doctor," she says. "He'll be working at the Point Lookout hospital part-time and is thinking of starting his own practice in Defiance."

Wow! Doc is a real MD! I thought Doc was just a nickname he'd picked up while in the military working as a medic. So much for knowing anything about him. I guess there are things he never got around to telling me. But then again, talking was not our main occupation when we ended up alone together.

"I think it's a great idea," Lisa continues. "Defiance could definitely use a general practitioner."

As Ice and Lisa are called away, Everest asks, "Do you wanna go over and see him?"

I shake my head vigorously.

"Why not?"

"'Cause I refuse to be like my mother." My tone is more abrupt than I want it, but my friend gets the message.

He was around to see what a spectacle my mother made of herself after Dad left. She'd always turned a blind eye to the Sweet butts and all the affairs he'd had when he was married to her.

Somehow he'd managed to convince her that when you married a biker, that was the norm. In hindsight, it probably was at the time, but it tore her apart every time he came back after a crazy night smelling of another woman's perfume.

After a while, he started staying away more often. As far as we were concerned, the parents acted as if everything was normal.

"Daddy is away a lot because he needs to travel," they would say. If my sisters fell for it, I sure didn't. I knew better, 'cause often enough, walking back from school, I would see him ride through town while he was supposed to be away.

Of course, I never said anything to my mother. I could see in her eyes that she knew already and was struggling to keep it together.

Then he stopped coming home altogether. Soon after, Mom found out there was another woman carrying his jacket and his child. That's when she lost it. When Dad would come around to see us, she would go half insane.

She cajoled, pleaded, begged, threatened and then begged again. Sometimes she managed to coax him into staying the night. That was the worst. Like rubbing salt into her wound since he never stayed more than one night.

Almost two decades have past, and still, just thinking about it makes me shudder. Everest studies my expression gravely. I know he understands. He was there. He saw it all. She loved my dad so much that she had no pride left. She even confronted him in public at the clubhouse.

So no, I don't want to turn into such a horrible mess. I will never, ever, beg a man to stay with me. I will never, ever, try, as my mother did, to use a child as leverage to keep a man.

"Guilt shouldn't be the cement that keeps a family together," I tell him.

He nods but doesn't give up.

"Come on, Bunny, you know me better than that. I'm not telling you to guilt him into coming back to you. What I'm saying is he has a right to know."

I think about it and I'm not sure.

As if reading my mind, Everest argues with my silence.

"If not for him, then you should do it for the kid. You know, so that the child has a least an opportunity to have a father."

Thankfully his pleading is interrupted by the first salvo of fireworks. We lie on the sand and look up to the sky. The show is lovely. I watch the colorful bursts and join the "aww" and "oohs" of the crowd.

At the end of the show, Birdy has vanished. I wonder who she's gone with, but if I want to know I'll have to ask her myself since no one noticed her leaving.

Everest walks me to my car at the hotel lot. Birdy's car is still there. She probably found someone to take her to the party at the MC and will come for her ride tomorrow.

Thankfully I don't have to work for the rest of the week. I'm so tired, I will probably sleep away most of it.

"You're not coming to the party, are you?" Everest asks.

I laugh and admit the idea of joining a loud bunch of drunk bikers to celebrate the passing of the old year and welcome the new one is not tempting, at all, right now.

"Nope, what I long for is a warm bath with delicious smelling salt and then I'll sleep or watch a silly show on television."

"So you're gonna be okay all by yourself?"

"Sure, and you know, Mom and Kitty are just a phone call away." I reassure him. "What about you?"

"I'll probably turn in early as well," he says. "I'm going to Miami in the morning."

"Going to see Kristal?"

He nods and a smile illuminates his face at the very mention of her name.

"How is she?" I want to take back my question. His girlfriend is doing time in a correctional facility, and I know it's difficult for both of them. It's especially hard on him since he put her there. He tries to catch up by going to visit her every chance he gets.

"She's doing okay," he says. "All things considered, she got a good deal and should be released soon."

"Oh, that's great news!" I squeeze his hand and put a kiss on his cheek. "Well, tell her I'm happy she's holding up and look forward to seeing her again."

"Will do." He closes my door and waits for me to drive away.

I roll down my window and say, "You'll see, this year will be the best ever!"

He laughs at my burst of optimism, but I'm convinced it's going to get better. At least for him, since his girlfriend is getting out of jail. And as far as I'm concerned, things will really get interesting.

I smile to myself and pat my belly.

Yep, I'm not alone. I have a fabulous family. I have incredible friends. I can make this work with or without Doc.

But I would rather do it with him.

7

BUNNY

"Is it okay if I leave now?" I ask my boss.

He looks at his watch and frowns as if my request was totally unreasonable.

"If you must." His condescending tone makes me want to scream, but it's my fault. When I started, I never counted my hours. It took me a few months to realize my efforts would never be acknowledged or appreciated.

Now that I am aware of how self-centered the man is, a course correction is in order. This gal won't be caught volunteering unpaid overtime. Nope, I won't be taken for granted.

Well, that's what I keep telling myself, but today, again, I got sucked into helping him finish a report due a week ago. I could very well do his job, but since I'm not getting his salary, I don't see why I should.

My hours are nine to five, not nine to six or seven. So now that it's almost six, I'm going. An annoyed sigh chases me out the door as I close it. I refuse to be lured back to work. I don't care. I won't hold his hand any longer. At least, not tonight.

Yesterday, Everest gave me an ultimatum. Either I went to talk to

Doc tonight or he would ride to the Knights' compound himself over the weekend and give him the news.

The drive to Defiance is short, but once I arrive, I get lost. Everest's direction are a bit too fuzzy for me. I drive around and can't seem to find the road to the Old Macmillan's farm.

I'm about to give up when I pass an inviting looking diner. Neon signs flash the words *Trucker's Heaven*. Funny to run into a *Trucker's Heaven* after working at *Biker's Heaven*. The old place is full. Maybe someone will know their way around and help me find the right road.

Also, I badly need to stop. When I drive, it's like the baby sits directly on my bladder.

As soon as I push the door, a woman's voice calls out my name. "Bunny, it's so nice to see you again!"

I turn and look at the waitress coming to me with opened arms. It takes a couple of second before I recognize her. In my memory, Belle has this huge mess of blond curls. It's like a work of art that always looks fabulous, as if she just stepped out of some fancy hair dresser's chair to walk onto a movie set.

Today her hair is covered by some sort of net and tied up in a bun on top of her head. It's probably more practical for work and it shows her lovely face in a new light.

"Belle Hutchinson," I answer returning her hug. "It's been ages." I take a step back to get a better look at her. "You're looking amazing. You haven't changed a bit!"

She laughs and points to my belly. "I see you're picking up where I left off!"

"Indeed, I am!" I concede. "How is your baby boy?"

"He's good and growing way too fast for my taste." She beams as she tells me all about little Chris.

I count back in my head, but can't figure out his age. Five or six? Seeing her brings flash memories of high school and her passionate relationship with her boyfriend. Peter ... I can't remember his last name. He was a sweet boy. We were all friends before heroin became his only love. He died of an overdose just when Belle realized she was pregnant.

"What brings you to this neck of the wood?" Belle asks.

"I'm looking for the Old Macmillan farm," I tell her.

"Oh, you're here on business to visit the Knights."

"Sort of." I do not volunteer any further information. I'll let Doc decide what he wants to say to his club.

After visiting the facilities, I take notes of the directions which are more specific than the ones I had before. Must be something gender related cause she doesn't say, *turn left after an eighth of a mile* but turn left at *the second light after the pizza place...*

We exchange phone numbers and promise to call each other soon. As I leave, she asks, "How's Everest?"

"He's good," I say. "He's gone to Miami to pick up his girlfriend. He's really excited she's moving in with him."

Belle's mouth forms a pretty little *O* giving away her surprise. Her eyes run up and down from my belly to my face and I can read her mind.

"Oh, no, he's not the dad," I say and rush out the door before she asks for more.

"Don't be a stranger, now," she calls out as I walk away.

Belle's directions get me to Knights territory within a few minutes. I park my car next to three others and step out toward the main building. The tables and benches next to it lead me to believe it's the clubhouse.

Before I get to it, a woman comes out of the building.

"Can I help you?" she asks with a big smile. She's wearing the same color apron Belle was wearing at the diner. The embroidery on the lapel identifies her as Holly.

"Yes, I'm looking for Doc."

"Sure, let me walk you to his place," she says pointing to the direction I just came from. "I'm on my way out, but it's just by the parking lot."

"You work at Trucker's Heaven with Belle?"

Holly smiles and frowns at the same time studying my face. "Do I know you?"

"I'm an old friend. Just saw her there at work. I had lost my way." My explanation doesn't help cause Holly looks even more puzzled. "It's the uniform ..." and then Holly gets it and laughs.

"I was wondering if you're psychic or something." Before I can point out it's observation, she shows me the door to a building I walked passed earlier and says, "In there. His room is the second one on the left."

I pause to gather my courage and make my way in what must have been living quarters for the staff when the farm was operating. A hallway runs through the entire length of the construction, and I can count a half dozen doors on each side.

I knock on the second one on the left and a woman's voice answers, "Yeah."

Opening the door to a large bedroom, the first thing that hits me is the smell. It's all Doc. I don't know what it is, his shaving soap or his shampoo, but the smell hits me in the gut. It's manly and clean and so delicious. I wish I had brought an empty jar to capture it and take it home.

And then I see her, laying on the bed with a book in her hand. She's the girl who was riding with him on New Year's Eve. Her Goth look is even more impressive from close up. Everything about her is dark, as if she's absorbed all the light around her and turned it into gloom. Black hair, dark clothes, charcoal eyes, almost purple lips.

"What do you want?" Even her voice is dark. Angry.

"I was looking for Doc."

"Well, you can see, he's not here." She shrugs and looks back to her book.

"Know when he'll be back?"

"Nope," she answers without even looking up.

I dig through my bag for a piece of paper and a pen. I write my name and home number on it. I want to give it to her, but she's back in her book making a big show of ignoring my presence.

So instead of handing it to her, I slip the paper on the bedside table underneath the alarm clock.

"Could you please tell him Bunny came by?" I ask. "I would appreciate it if he could call me."

"Uh uh."

I turn and close the door behind me. I hold myself together until I reach my car. I drive away as sedately as possible so nobody watching can see how upset I am and then I stop on a dirt road. Only there do I let my rage explode.

As if the frustration from work were not enough, I had to run into that arrogant bitch. I bang my fist against the steering wheel and scream out my anger.

I'm not sure whom I'm angriest at.

Everything and everyone.

I'm angry at myself first for getting caught. I was so sure we had never been careless, but I should have known better. Even in the heat of the moment, the woman needs to check that protection is used.

I'm angry at Doc for making me believe he cared and would come back for me. I wasn't asking for promises. He shouldn't have given me hope if it was to snatch it away so quickly.

And finally, I'm so, so mad at Everest for making me look for Doc.

The last thing I needed was the humiliation of facing his new girl. Because she has to be his new girl. Who else but a girlfriend would be in his room, lying on his bed while he's out?

At the end of the day, I know it's all my fault.

With each kiss, I felt love.

With each caress, I heard a promise.

I was so sure I wasn't dreaming, but I should have known better. Why do I hear more than what is being said. I need to listen better.

No words were ever used to plan for tomorrows. It was all in my head.

8

DOC

All I want is a shower and my bed. It's been a hell of a day, most of it spent patching up the results of yet another drunk driver. At least he hit a bus, and not a minivan. Still we spent the day patching up kids.

No one protested my choice of anesthetic—none. The head nurse's normal frown lifted a bit, just enough to be called a smile. That smile made my day.

When I step through the door of my room Raven's there. Of course she is, reading a book on my bed. Damn it.

"Hey, Doc," she asks looking up from one of the romance novels she loves. "How was your day? How are you?"

"What are you doing here?" Yeah, what the fuck gives her the right to try and claim my space, my time… especially after a shift like that?

Oblivious to the bite of my tone she purrs, "Oh, poor baby." She gets on her knees and closes her book. "What if gave you a back rub?"

I roll my eyes at her and point to the door.

"Goodnight, Raven." I'm in no mood to deal with her nonsense.

"Why are you so mean to me?" she asks with a pitiful tone.

She looks so miserable and unhappy that I soften my tone to tell her, "I'm not. You don't listen."

"Yes, I do listen. You said rest and calm. Can I stay if I promise to be real quiet?" she pleads, dropping her book on my nightstand and walking toward me.

I point to the door again.

"Nope! Right now, I need to be alone." The girl is trying my patience.

She pouts and relents. "Fine, I'll go."

As soon as the door slams behind her I strip and get the shower running. It takes at least a full minute before the hot water kicks in. I step back into my room to grab a towel and laugh. She's left her book on my nightstand. I shake my head and curse under my breath. The girl is impossible.

While under the shower, I wonder what to do about her. The options are limited. The only way I can shake her loose is behaving like an ass with her. I told her I wasn't interested, but she doesn't get it. Why do women have to be so complicated? Not just her, most women.

The scalding water conjures memories of showers taken with Bunny in her tiny studio by the university. One thing I loved about Bunny was that she was not complicated. Everything about her was easy.

When I close my eyes, I see her radiant smile and magnificent curves. The swell of her belly and the gentle wiggling of her breast when I entered her with slow strokes.

Shit, I've gotten myself all worked up and there's no one to finish the job. Well, no one I want ... cause right now, Raven is standing by the bathroom door carrying a six pack of my favorite beer and two frosted glasses.

Without taking a towel, I storm out of the shower.

"What the fuck are you doing here?"

My bark doesn't appear to scare her one bit. It's like she doesn't hear it. Her eyes are riveted to my erection. She's looking at it like a mongoose stares at a snake and I feel the absurd urge to cover myself.

When I do, she looks up to my face with a malicious smile.

"I forgot my book," she says. "And I thought maybe you'd want to share one of these..."

Okay, this is it. One jerk coming right up.

I snatch one beer from her, open it and take a big gulp. I get closer and belch in her face. She winces and takes a step back. I follow her and grab her book from the table.

"What part of *I wanna be alone* did you not understand?"

"I thought ... I thought..." she almost stutters unable to finish her sentence.

"I didn't ask you to think," I snarl back. "I asked you to get the fuck out of my room."

"But ..."

"Read my lips, Raven. I. Want. You. Out. Now!"

This is the last straw for her. Her expression changes. The beaten puppy turns into a rabid dog, almost foaming at the mouth, she yells at me.

"You're just like the rest of them. Nothing but a bastard. You took advantage of me so I would show you around when no one else would talk to you and now, now you're throwing me out like yesterday's trash! I hate you!"

I catch her arm and attempt to pull her to the door but she resists. She's surprisingly strong for such a light weight. She twists her arm to escape my grip and bends towards the table to grab a piece of paper that must have fallen from her book. As soon as she has it, she raises her arms as if surrendering.

"Don't you dare touch me," she yells walking backward in direction of the door. "I hate you. I hope you rot in hell forever. I hope your dick freezes and falls off..."

That last bit has me laughing out loud. That infuriates her. Like a raving lunatic, she yells as she retreats into the hallway were a few doors have opened. Some of the brothers who live in the building step out of their rooms to find out what all the ruckus is about.

Dragon stands in the doorway directly across from mine—naked and grinning ear to ear. Fuck me sideways—his dick is tattoed—just thinking of how painful that must have been, I wince. His favorite Sweet butt, dressed in her birthday suit slides her head between his arm and the door frame to have a look at the show.

Raven continues to curse and I have to admit, she has a very extensive vocabulary for a girl her age. Her images are vividly disturbing and I feel sorry for the man who will fall in love with her. He'll need nerves of steel and a welder's mask to watch her blow. For his sake, I hope she's as passionate in the sack.

But right now, Raven is out of control. She doesn't seem to care that she's acting like a mad woman, putting on a show for the benefit of way too many MC members. The club lives on gossip. The story will be reported and amplified for a few days until another juicy piece of information makes it yesterday's news.

When she finally exits the building, Dragon winks at me and says, "If I were you, I'd lock my door tonight. She's mad enough to come back in the middle of the night armed and dangerous."

I nod and realize it's probably very wise advice. Good thing the key is on the door. While I'm at it, I close the metal window shutters, as well. No need to tempt fate by letting things get out of control.

After finishing my beer, put the rest of the forgotten pack in the mini-fridge and brush my teeth.

I hit the sack, shut down the light.

Three seconds later, I'm dead to the world.

9

BUNNY

I'm so, so, so tired. I hate the evening shift. Driving home, I remember I have nothing but healthy food in the house. Who cares? I don't want healthy food right now, I need sugar, grease, downright sinful indulgence.

Instead of driving home and rolling into bed, I stop for groceries.

Nothing like ice cream and blueberries to paste the cracks of a shattered heart. My plan is to sit in front of the television and eat myself into a stupor. If ice cream doesn't do the trick, I'll turn to chocolate.

As soon as I turn the corner to my street, I realize my plans are going to have to wait. There's one truck and two bikes in my driveway. One is my father's Harley.

The second I'm parked, Earplugs rushes out of my house with a gun in his hand. I feel like an iron fist closing around my heart. This can't be good news. Despite the large smile he pastes on his face when he recognizes me, I'm filled with dread.

Earplugs tucks his gun away in the back of his belt and takes my grocery bags. He's a sweet guy who should get his patch soon enough. For more than a year, he's been my father's trainee, so to speak. His favorite prospect.

Before Baby Jack was born a few months ago, Daniel, Earplugs's real name, was the son Dad always dreamed of having. My sisters and I were ambivalent about him. On one hand we were jealous. On the other, we were happy Dad had someone devoted to him. It never hurts to have a true friend looking out for you when you're in his line of business.

"Brains?" I ask using my father's nickname in the MC. Earplugs nods and follows me as I rush into my house.

"How bad?"

"We're not sure," he says looking into the grocery bags "Why don't you go see him. I'll put this away."

I throw my handbag on the table as I run past toward the bedroom. Toward Dad. Lobster and Waxer are standing by the bed tending, to my father. He's flat on his back, white as my sheets. On the floor by the bed, most of my towels have been thrown in a pile, soaked in blood.

Lobster catches me watching the towels and tries to reassure me. "Most of the blood's not his," he says. "The guy he was fighting fell on him and he was bleeding like a pig."

I take a step closer to the bed and notice that someone had the good idea to rip out my shower curtain to protect the bed. Sending a silent thanks to whomever was so thoughtful, I examine my father's body.

Other than the wound beneath the blood soaked towel, Waxer's presses tightly, he looks fine. Or fine as can be, anyway. There are a few cuts but nothing significant.

"Why did you bring him here?"

The two men turn their eyes away and remain silent. Their cowardliness infuriates me. Nothing in my tone implied I was questioning their decision. I'm asking a simple question. What I want to know is why they didn't drive him to the clubhouse where they have a serious first aid kit, or better yet, to the hospital.

"It's a bullet wound," Earplugs explains.

So much for taking him to the hospital. The doctors would need to report it, and the club probably doesn't need to wave any red flag at the authorities.

There's only so much Everest can sweep under the rug.

Lobster's face is redder than usual, almost crimson. Staring at the point of his boots, he mumbles, "We figured that since the bullet went through, as soon as he would stop bleeding, he would be fine."

"But the most important thing is that no one will come looking for him in this house," Earplugs says. "Before he passed out, Brains told me the deed was still in your grandma's name. So if anyone comes to investigate, they may go next door." He points at my mother's house through the window. "But they won't come here."

"Unless you leave your bikes and the truck in front of my door," I retort.

Waxer curses under his breath, "Oh fuck, you're right. I never thought about that."

It doesn't surprise me. These two guys are not the sharpest knives in the MC's drawers. Yet they're loyal as fuck to my dad. Enough that he clearly trusts them with his life.

"Is there a chance someone will come looking for him?" I ask to no one in particular. My eyes are on my father whose breathing seems labored suddenly. My heart is in my throat. I don't want to go against his orders, but if it's comes to a choice between him dead and him alive and in jail, I'll take the second option.

"Yeah, one of the guys from the other crew got away and he's probably figured out who we are," Lobster confesses.

"Then you'd better move the truck and the bikes quickly."

"I think I should stay," Earplugs states gravely.

"Yeah, yeah, sure." The truth is I'm grateful for his offer and I'll be more comfortable with him around than I would be with the two other brutes.

Earplugs takes Waxer's place by my father's side, pressing on the towel while I go out with the other men to open the garage door. They push Dad's ride in and leave with the second bike and the truck.

"You're gonna be okay with the kid?" Waxer asks.

"Yeah, don't worry. I'll call if I need help."

Happy to see them gone, I return to my room and pull a chair to the side of the bed so Daniel can sit. We both observe my father's heavy breathing in silence. I find a place on the other side of the bed and proceed to wipe away all traces of blood from my father's face and torso. I want to finish undressing him to make sure there's nothing wrong with his legs, but I'm afraid to move him.

I dig up a clean sheet and a comforter from the other room and cover him. It seems absurd to keep him warm. After all, this is Florida. It's not that cold. Yet, I know it's the right thing to do.

Once he's bundled up, I stay idle at the foot of the bed, wondering what to do next.

I'm lost and grateful for the prospect's presence even though the concern on his face mirrors my own anxiety.

The young man looks at me and sighs.

"He's gonna be fine," I say tentatively. I'm not certain whom I'm trying to convince.

"Of course," he answers. "I'd feel a heck of a lot better if we could show him to a doctor."

I shake my head and then a lights turn on finally.

"Ah doctor, of course."

Earplugs looks at me as if I've gone suddenly crazy.

"Daniel," I ask. "Do you know the way to the Knight's place?"

"Yeah, of course. They've taken over the big abandoned farm house on the outskirt of Defiance."

"Good." I take a deep breath. "I want you to go there and ask for Doc."

"Doc?" He frowns at me.

"Yeah, he's one of their new members," I explain. "You take Dad's bike, go there and find him. When you do, bring him back here."

"What if he doesn't wanna come?"

"He will," I claim with more conviction than I really have. "You tell him Bunny desperately needs a favor."

I move to the other side of the bed and replace Earplugs. Soon enough, I hear him kick Dad's ride alive and roll away.

"It's just me and you, Dad," I tell him. He doesn't react to the sound of my voice. I wish he could open his eyes and say something. All alone with him now, I resist the temptation to lift the towel and check the bleeding has really stopped. But then the towel would be soaked if it hadn't. Anyway, I'm too scared about what would happen if I looked, so I don't.

The only thing I can do now is pray.

Pray that even if my child's dad has moved on, he still likes me enough to come when I call for his help.

10

DOC

Jolted awake by powerful knocks on the door, my first thought is I'm going to strangle Raven. The girl never quits. I pull my pillow over my head. If I ignore her long enough, she'll go away. She doesn't. I think a spanking is in order.

As I get out of bed, the knocks grow louder.

Fuck. She can't be the one at the door.

"Doc! Open the damned door. It's an emergency," Prince's voice is loud. He's probably startled everyone awake by now.

I unlock the door. And yeah, most of the other doors of the hallway are open. Again!

Dragon's Sweet butt is standing by the door with a just-fucked hairdo. She's giggling.

"Wow, this is better than the afternoon soaps!"

I motion for Prince to come in. He does and looks at my empty bed. "What's with the locked door?"

"Because Raven's crazy."

Dragon's girl follows him to my door.

"Raven?" Prince asks puzzled.

"Don't ask!" I answer.

From the other side of the hallway Dragon calls out. "Get your ass back in bed or else ..." He leaves his sentence unfinished, but it's clear it's not a real threat. The tone of his voice belies the content of the words. If anything, he sounds like he's making a promise.

"Sorry guys, got to go," she says as she retreats into Dragon's crib and shuts the door behind her. A few seconds later, we hear her laugh and him growl.

The sound show ends as Prince pulls in another guy and closes my door behind them.

"This is Earplugs. He's a Tornado prospect," Prince explains as if I didn't recognize the logo. "He says Bunny sent him for you."

I give the man a look over and notice that part of his tee shirt is covered with brownish spots.

My blood runs cold. Fuck, I sure hope it's not hers!

"Bunny? Is she okay?" Despite the fact I bark my question out, the prospect stands his ground.

"Yeah, yeah, she's fine. It's Brains," he answers.

"That's her dad," Prince explains. "He's the Sergeant-at-Arms of the Tornadoes."

"What's with her father?" Clearly the man's injured and needs a doctor to patch him up. What I want is more specifics about the wound.

Earplugs gets it. He points to his waist and says, "One bullet, in and out." The young man's expression tells me he sincerely cares for the man. "It looks clean, but he's lost a lot of blood."

"How long ago?" I ask jumping into the jeans I abandoned by the door of the bathroom earlier.

"About a couple of hours now. Is that bad?"

I shrug. It all depends. There's no way I can answer his question without knowing more, which I will after I look at the wound.

"Do you want me to come along?" Prince asks.

Pulling out my emergency kit from the closet, I turn to Earplugs. "Is he in a safe place?"

"Yeah. He's at Bunny's house in Point Lookout. Before he passed out, he asked us to take him to her. He said no one would come look for him there."

"So, someone's looking for him?" Prince states matter-of-factly.

"Yeah, not the cops but ..." I can see Earplugs is uncomfortable telling us more.

"Listen, kid," Prince snarls. " We can't go in there blind. If you want our help we need intel."

While I finish putting my boots on, Earplugs shifts his weight from one foot to the other and comes to a decision. "Let's go," he says. "It's safe enough that I left Bunny alone with him, but you can sure come along."

I grab my bag and we follow him out.

"You've heard of the Bikers dream?" he asks. Prince nods energetically. "Well, we found the lab where they make it and torched it."

Prince lets out an impressed whistle. Takes balls to torch an opponent's base of operation. "Cool move."

"What kind of drug is it?" It's probably not relevant to the condition Bunny's father is in, but now I'm curious.

"The sort that fucks with your head and makes you believe you can fly," Prince tells me as we walk to our rides. "They've been feeding it to the underground racers all over Florida and the body count is scary."

We start our bikes and that puts an end to our conversation. I know enough for now.

Earplugs takes the lead and turns in the direction of Point Lookout. As we ride, my mind races ahead to Bunny.

I've missed her so fucking much. I feel her getting closer. It's only a few miles between Defiance and Point Lookout, but my craving for her grows by the minute. I can't understand why I waited all this time to go to her. I should have gone and grabbed her the very day I came back.

Now that I'm going to see her, I want her badly. She's like an addictive drug I wouldn't wanna give up.

Of course, I have competition now. Well, too bad for Everest. He'll be out of the picture tonight. The woman needs to know there's no such thing as a free lunch. I'll make it clear that my help comes with a price.

She wants it.

Hell no, she needs it.

She'll get it and be mine again.

Yeah, that will be the deal, and if memory serves me right, coming in my bed will be no hardship for her.

I want her back and nothing will stand in my way.

Nothing at all.

11

BUNNY

The minutes tick away and I pray Earplugs has found Doc. They should be riding back. The clock says he's been gone less than forty-five minutes, but it feels like hours.

My father is still pale and his breathing is a bit less labored. Unless I've grown used to the sound of it. My arms are sore, but I keep pressure on the wound. I want to rest my forehead on my hands. I'm so tired, I almost fall asleep.

Moving to the edge of my seat, I adopt the most uncomfortable position I can to stay awake. Why didn't I ask Earplugs to get Birdy first? Because I didn't think. Because it would have been a bad idea. Birdy can't deal with the sight of blood.

Several times my heart races as I hear the roar of engines, but each time it's a false alarm. The engines roar and pass by, the sounds quickly fade away. Has there always been so much traffic on my street?

Finally the distinctive sound of the Harley engines come to die by my door. I hear low voices. The garage door opens and closes. There's a reason why my father likes Earplugs; he thinks. Not such a common occurrence with most bikers.

The door that leads from the garage to the kitchen opens and I hear Daniel's voice. "Over there."

My heart races. It beats so strongly, it's like a bird trying to fly from its cage. It's my father, it's Doc, it's the baby, it's the job I hate ... my life is in shambles and there's nothing I can do but watch it fall apart.

"Holy fuck!"

Even though I have my back to the door, I'm guessing Doc is having the same reaction I had looking at the towels on the floor. Before I have a chance to say anything, Earplugs explains once more, "It's not his blood."

Doc is now inches from me. So close I can feel his heat. He's always been warm blooded. I look up to him, and he ignores me. First, he stares at my father, and then he finally acknowledge my presence.

Not in a good way.

"Scram!"

He punctuates his order with a shooing motion . I want to protest, but I bite my tongue. Now is not the time to argue with him. I stand without letting go of my father. In a second, a powerful hand comes to replace mine on the towel. The hand belongs to Prince. He nods at me and says, "Your heard the man. Go wait in the other room."

I move away slowly and Doc still doesn't look at me. He's busy opening the very large bag he's put on my chair.

"Door!" Prince barks.

So much for watching from the living room.

Earplugs gently takes me by the arm and softly closes the door behind me.

"Come on, Bunny." He leads me to my rocking chair. I gratefully plop myself down and wrap my arms around my belly. I'm cold. I'm tired. I'm grumpy. I feel useless and stupid.

I need to do something. If I don't, I'm going to go crazy.

Earplugs's stomach grumbles and inspires me. I should cook.

"Hungry?" I ask.

Earplugs shakes his head and grins. "That loud?"

"Yeah, but it's a good thing. Let me feed you. I'll make soup. I have some chicken. That's perfect, I'll make broth and maybe Daddy will be able to have some when he wakes up..." I'm rambling, but I don't care and Earplugs doesn't seem to mind. The promise of food brought an ear to ear smile on his face.

Most men are easy that way.

He opens the kitchen door for me. I get bread, mustard, and cold cuts. He takes those while I pull out carrots, onions and the whole chicken I had planned to roast tomorrow.

While I grab for my grandmother's largest pot and fill it with water, Earplugs prepares a huge sandwich. By the time I find the cutting board and meat cleaver, he's gulped it down and peeling the carrots.

Who knew he was so domestic? I chop the chicken into small pieces and toss them into the pot as I go along.

"Now I know not to get on your bad side when you're armed with a knife." Prince stands by the kitchen door. His tone is mocking, but judging by the look on Daniel's face, I must have looked fearsome as I let all my rage and frustration out on the poor bird.

"How is he?" I ask.

"Doc says he's gonna be okay." Earplugs and I let out a deep sigh of relief. "He wants to talk to you."

"Dad? He's awake?"

"Nah, Doc."

"Oh," I'm disappointed. I was so hoping Dad would come around. But I should know better than to be overly optimistic. "Sure, let me wash my hands and I'll be right over."

While I move to the sink, my father's favorite prospect takes over. "Don't worry, I've got this."

Prince waits and walks me to my bedroom. His hand on the handle and staring at the bulge at my mid-section. "It's his, isn't it?" he whispers.

For a second I hesitate. Can I make believe I don't understand what he's asking about? Nope, his gaze is too serious for that. So instead of lying, I nod.

"And he doesn't know?"

I shake my head. Incredibly my answer seems to make him happy. I think it's the first time I see a smile illuminate his face.

"Then it's gonna all be good."

I wish I could share his optimism.

I want to ask him why he feels this way, but he doesn't leave me time. He opens the door and pushes me in.

The room is dim. The only light comes from the bathroom door left ajar. In the penumbra, I can hardly see my father's features. The noise of the water running covers the sound of his breathing.

"Gimme a minute." Dad doesn't react to the sound of Doc's voice calling out from the bathroom.

The same doesn't hold true for me.

There's always been something about Doc's voice. It's deep and velvety, so smooth, it made me swoon. Tonight I still feel the shiver but somehow, it's not the same.

12

DOC

I take twice as much time as I need to wash my hand and then again to dry them. Being in Bunny's bathroom is both heaven and hell. The room smells like her. I want to bury my face in the bathrobe hanging on the door. I don't. The robe won't cut it. I want to breathe in the smell of her skin when I kiss her neck. I want to inhale her fragrance as I nip her skin and dig my fingers in her hair.

Slowly I find my way to the door and return to her bedroom. The light is at my back and that's perfect. Bunny can't see my expression as I observe her.

She deserves to be kept on edge. She didn't wait for me. And fuck it, if I'm unfair. The green demon of jealousy has been shredding my guts for weeks.

Bunny stands by the bed, gently caressing her father's cheek. There's so much tenderness in her gesture, it makes me sad.

What sort of a bastard am I to resent even the affection she has for her dad? A possessive one.

"He'll need to lay low for a few days," I declare. My tone is all business. "But he's gonna be fine."

She turns toward me and whispers, "Thank you, Doc."

A few steps and she's right in front of me, she stands on her toes and puts her lips to my cheek. "Thank you so much ..."

That brotherly kiss is sweet, but it's like a slap in the face. I don't take crumbs. The gesture infuriates me. I want more, so much more.

If she thinks that's how she's going to pay her debt, she's sadly mistaken. I reach out and pull her against me, a tug on her hair and her mouth is right under mine. I pull a little harder and her lips open with a moan. The very sound of it hits me full blast. Who cares if it's pain or pleasure? I don't. The only thing that matters is that she's in my arms again and her soft body is molded against mine.

My hands explore the familiar territory. I love that it's curvier than before. Her breasts are fuller and that fills me with joy. As I touch her, smothered sounds escape from her mouth.

She's always been loud but not today.

My Bunny's holding back.

She doesn't know that her father is so loaded with sedative, I could probably fuck her standing against the bed, make her scream and he wouldn't stir.

"Oh, Bunny," I whisper in her ear pressing her against the wall. The swell of her belly is not an illusion and there is no mistaking its origin.

I don't care.

She's mine no matter what.

I'll take her, even full with another man's child.

As soon as she begins to kiss me back, I let go of her mouth. She makes a little sound, like a protest as I pull away and move her head until her face rests on my chest. We both catch our breath and in the distance I hear the roar of two bikes rolling away. A silent thanks goes to Prince. He's convinced the annoying kid to leave with him.

I break the silence. "We need to talk."

Bunny stiffens and tries to pull away.

I hold her back. "Not here. Out there."

I point toward the next room and holding her hand, make her leave her father's bedside. There's nothing she can do for him now.

As soon as the door opens, I'm distracted by a fabulous smell of food. I'm starving. Now that I think of it, I remember Raven's beer was my dinner.

"Did you eat?" I ask her.

She shakes her head, "I forgot."

"In your condition, that's unreasonable." My answer comes out harsher than I want and she tries to pull away again.

I hold fast and she looks up to me.

"Why should you care?" Her expression is puzzled and sad. So sad, watching it hurts.

"Because from now on you're mine."

Fuck, now that sounds like a threat and that's not how I wanted it to come out.

"What do you mean?" Her confusion is real.

"There's a price to pay for saving your father."

"And what would that be?" Sadness is turning into defiance.

"You." Her mouth opens in a perfect little *O*. "You're the price. From now on, you're mine."

All my determination came out with those words. There will be no discussion. She's mine. Period.

Her disbelief is written all over her face as she points an accusing finger at me.

"You, you, you ..." she can't find her words and shakes her head. "Of all the arrogant bastards I've known ..." She stops and takes a deep breath. "You think you can disappear and then ..."

That's when she loses it.

She's laughing hysterically and sobbing at the same time.

First she pushes me away, and then her fists close on my tee shirt. She holds on to me for dear life and shakes her head.

She's not making much sense, but I won't hold that against her. It's probably the aftershock of her father's injury, that and the hormones.

Whatever it is, she's given herself up to the maelstrom of emotions raging through her and is drowning in the whirlpool.

I pick her up and notice another door which goes to the living room. I push it open. It leads to a smaller bedroom with bunk beds. I frown and then remember it was her grandma's house. Looks like at some point the woman had her grandchildren for sleepovers.

I lay Bunny on one of the lower bunks and sit next to her. She keeps on rambling incoherently for a bit and when she finally calms down, she only has one question.

"Why?"

Uncertain of what she's asking, I caress her face and hush her. "Get some sleep, sweetheart, we'll talk when you're rested."

She nods gravely and closes her eyes. Soon enough her breathing is regular. When I'm sure she's asleep, I stand and take the patchwork quilt from the upper bunk to cover her.

Leaving the door open, I make my way to the kitchen. By the stove there's a note: *"Sandwich in the fridge. Don't forget the broth."*

I take a bite from the sandwich and lift the lid from the pot. There's enough liquid to let it simmer for another hour. I lower the heat and look in on my patient. The man is lucky. It could have been a lot worse.

After checking on Bunny, I explore the rest of the house. The garage is an incredible mess. It looks like three generations of clutter has accumulated. Old wooden toys sit on shelves next to first generation video games which probably don't work anymore. Florida humidity will have them moldy and rusted away.

The washer and dryer stacked by the door remind me of the pile of bloody towels. Just in case anyone should come over, I start a load of laundry and go heavy on the bleach.

Once that's done, I retreat to the living room. Browsing through the book shelves, I find old photo albums. Finishing my sandwich at the table, I get acquainted with Bunny's family.

There's her childhood pictures with a younger version of Brains. He hasn't changed much. His hair line has receded and what's left went from jet black to salt and pepper. Still, he's in great shape for a man of his age. And Bunny, well Bunny's the spitting image of her grandma.

I'm not surprised the woman left her the house. That grand kid of hers is her ticket to immortality. It's as if she's cloned herself in her eldest granddaughter.

That's when I realize I didn't ask Bunny what gender the baby was. I hope it's a girl. It will be easier with a girl. I'm afraid if it's a boy, I'll be annoyed with him when I see the resemblance to the birth father.

I shrug away my worry. That's stupid.

I should know better. When it comes to nature versus nurture, nurture always wins.

13

BUNNY

The sound of two men talking wakes me. I'm disoriented. Why am I not in my bed?

And then I remember.

I sit up and listen to the voices arguing.

The conversation is all hushed, but there's no mistaking the anger in both men's voices. As I tiptoe to the door, I identify the voices.

Everest and Doc are having a verbal show-down.

Hidden in the room, I stop and debate with myself. Eavesdropping sounds a lot more fun than confronting them.

"There's no discussion. From now on, I'll take care of her." Doc is adamant.

"Do you hear me protesting?" The sarcasm in Everest's voice is subtle. You need to know him to realize it's there. My guess is, it's flying over Doc's head.

"So you're fine with my taking charge?" Incredulity tints his tone.

"If it's fine with Bunny, it's fine with me." Now Everest is dead serious.

"You're shitting me?" Doc sounds outraged. Interesting. It doesn't make any sense.

Why would Doc want Everest to argue with him? The only explanation is he's under the impression I'm back with Everest? If he's seen us around town, it wouldn't be an absurd assumption. That and the fact Doc most likely caught Everest coming in the front door with his own key to my house.

"Nah, I mean it. Bunny's her own woman."

That's one thing Everest has always been good about. Respecting women. He's bossy in bed, a master in his dungeon, but when it comes to everyday life, there's infinite respect for those he cares about. Men and women alike.

"What kind of a bastard are you?" Doc growls.

I'm about to open the door and put an end to this absurd discussion when Everest has a light bulb moment.

"Oh, fuck! You think I'm the father!"

There's a few seconds of silence and then Doc asks, almost civil, "You're not?"

"Uh uh." I imagine Everest's shaking his head, and am sorry I can't be a fly on the wall. I would so love to see Doc's face right this instant. He always prides himself to be a fair person. The guy who gives everyone a chance. Up to now, it was everyone but Everest.

"Shit, I'm sorry man," Doc says. "You know, I thought ..."

Everest laughs. "I get it, but no. Not mine."

"So whose is it?"

Even though I'd bet good money that Everest's answer is going to be something like *"Why don't you ask her?"* I won't take the chance of him spilling the beans. I push the door open noisily and observe those two alpha males as they turn to face me.

They are both magnificent specimen of their gender. Doc is way shorter than Everest, less bulky, but that's mainly where the difference ends. They are both protective, decent, caring humans, and I do love them both.

With time, my love for Everest has evolved. The ardent passion of a teenager became an almost brotherly tenderness. The bond between us is indisputable evidence that a man and a woman can be friends.

My affection for Doc is something altogether different. It started with a blaze. A spectacular fire, one so hot, I almost ran for fear of getting scorched. But Doc was patient, he waited and climbed over all my barricades. Being with him was heavenly, so much, that he won my total surrender.

Of course, once he had me at his mercy, the man vanished, leaving me wondering if it would be wiser to smother the embers or protect them.

Ignoring Doc's question -- even though they both know I have heard it -- I say, "So, you two have met."

Everest smiles and comes to hug me.

"Yeah, and I'm happy he was here to help yesterday."

I hug him back and concur. "Yes, Doc saved my father's life."

Doc observes the way we're touching and when Everest lets me go, he comes to me and wraps an arm around my waist to pull me against him. The gesture is so possessive, it makes me want to laugh.

Men are nothing but big apes with an irresistible urge to mark their territories. I look up to him and add, "And now he thinks he has a claim on me."

"Oh, does he, now?" Everest is laughing. "I'm guessing that's my cue to leave. You two have things to discuss in private."

I silently mouth "traitor" and watch him run away with a cocky smile on his face.

"How's Brains today?" I ask.

"Do you always call your father that?"

"Nah, sometimes I call him Dad," I admit. "But since his new Old Lady is younger than me, I think he likes it better when I use his road name."

"Oh, I see." Doc walks with me to doorway of my room and whispers, "He's doing well. We chatted a bit when he woke up earlier. He was feeling hungry enough to taste your chicken stock."

He walks me to my bed. A hand on my father's forehead reassures me. He's not feverish and his coloring is almost normal. He stirs when I touch him, but doesn't open his eyes.

I push my door closed behind us as we retreat to the living room, then make my way to the kitchen. My stomach demands food.

"Want something?" I ask. In my grandmother's house—well, my house now--I can't help but be hospitable. The good manners she drilled into me override my desire to bark at him.

"No, it's all good. I made myself eggs earlier. Thanks."

A clean pan and plate resting by the sink confirm he's been cooking and tidying. He's more orderly than I am. I make myself a bowl of cereal, and as I sit at the table, marvel at the fact it's the first time in ages that I actually look forward to food in the morning.

Doc takes the chair across from mine and asks, "Are you taking supplements?"

"Nope," I answer with my mouth full and watch him frown at me. Before he has a chance to protest, I hold out my hand to stop him. "Hey, I'm doing what I can. My health insurance just kicked in."

Doc rolls his eyes at me and sighs.

"You mean you haven't consulted at all?"

What part of no medical insurance did he not get? The man remains silent for a minute, his fingers nervously taping the table. "Can you get someone to watch over your dad today?"

"Nah, it's all good. I'm not working today."

He sighs again and talking very softly as if dressing a stubborn child, he says, "I'm taking you to the hospital to run a full exam."

I finish my cereals silently mulling over his proposal. "You really mean it?"

"What?"

"You're taking charge from now on?"

He nods. "I rarely say things I don't mean."

"Why?"

One corner of his lips twitch and he doesn't answer right away.

"You're a smart woman, I'm pretty sure you can figure it out."

He picks up my empty bowl and takes it to the kitchen. While he washes it, I pick up the old fashion phone and dial my mother's place. I'm in luck since Birdy picks up.

"Good morning, sunshine," I say. "Could you come over right away. I need you for a bit."

14

DOC

Point Lookout Hospital doesn't have the latest equipment for sonograms, but what is available will be adequate for what I need to do today.

Everest's paternity denial has my mind reeling. There was no reason for him to lie. He doesn't have anything to prove. Not to me. Furthermore, I'm certain I didn't intimidate him. Fuck, if we were to fight, there's no question who would come out on top. I'm now more comfortable with a scalpel than bare fists.

A technician is waiting for us in the examination room. I called ahead an hour ago and even though she was not happy with my request, she has everything ready when we arrive. We're a bit late cause drawing blood for the tests took longer than I anticipated.

The woman gives me a questioning glance as she helps Bunny climb onto the table. Usually the doctors don't bother to get their patients settled in.

"I'll take it from here," I tell her keeping the door open for her. She frowns. Yeah, it's her room, but I'm higher on the food chain. "I'll only be a few minutes." She hesitates, and I decide to go for the carrot instead of the stick. "And I'll owe you."

That's a deal maker. She shrugs and relents.

"Pull your tee shirt up and slide your pants down a bit," I tell Bunny.

"The least you could do is ask me nicely."

Her eyes are sparkling. Yeah! Sulky Bunny is gone.

To welcome Happy Bunny back, I play along. "My dearest Bunny, would you please be kind enough to oblige."

"Well, of course, Doctor."

Her eyes land on the monitoring device just as I squirt gel on her tummy. It's cold enough to make her squeal.

"Did you do this on purpose?" She shakes a finger at me. "Maybe I should ask for another doctor."

Her protest stops cold as she looks at the probe I'm holding. There's no reason for any apprehension, but she doesn't know that.

I press the tip of the probe against her tummy and glide it on the gel. In a second, the monitor comes alive and a wooshing sound fills the tiny room.

Her eyes are wide, and as the sound becomes more regular, she asks "Is that the heart beat?"

"Yep, loud and strong," I tell her as I move the probe around and get a feel for the position of the baby.

"That's good, right?" The anxiety in her voice melts my heart. She didn't avoid prenatal care on purpose. Poor baby couldn't afford it. It makes me wonder about the financial situation of the Tornadoes.

If the MC is affluent, Brains should have offered to help. After all, the man just became a father, he knows what a pregnancy cost... The other possibility is she and her dad don't talk much.

"Absolutely." I use my best doctor voice to tell what I'm doing as I play with the dials to get some measurements.

"So with this machine, you'll be able to tell if everything's all right?"

"If you give me the date of conception, I'll be able to compare my results with tables that show what a normal growth is like."

"Oh, I see." Her answer is almost a whisper.

"So?"

She stares at the black and white dots of the screen has if they held the secret of the universe.

"What if I couldn't give you an exact date?"

I roll my eyes at her. "Give me some sort of clue, something like the date of your last period."

She opens and closes her mouth like a fish out of water.

Patience is usually my strongest suit. My grandmother used to tell me that I reminded her of the ocean eating away a cliff. In her eyes, it was a good thing. "Pebble after pebble, the waves carve the way into the most resistant stones," she repeated.

But today all my patience has vanished. I suspect--or should I say hope-- I'm the father and I want an answer *now*.

"End of June," Bunny's voice is so low, I'm not sure I heard her right.

Three words, three knives in my heart. She conceived after I left. Fuck. The baby's not mine.

"So your last periods were at the end of June?"

Somehow, I control my voice. My tone is detached, professional, almost cold. I hate myself for being such a stupid fool. I should have let the technician conduct the exam. I should have ... Bunny catches my hand and shakes her head.

Looking right in my eyes, she clarifies her answer. "No. What I meant is the date of conception was either June twenty-eight or twenty-nine."

I freeze, and for a few seconds, I forget how to breathe. Her news hits me in the stomach like an iron fist.

The kid is mine.

My mind goes back to that crazy weekend we spent locked up in her studio, only leaving her bed to open the door to the pizza or Thai food delivery. I knew at the time I wouldn't be back for weeks and wanted to get my fill of her before I left.

But I couldn't.

I acted like a real bastard 'cause when I ran out of condoms, instead of rushing out to get a new box, I continued to make love to her only thinking of my urges. A bastard with a total disregard of the possible consequences.

And here I am now, looking at the perfect profile of the consequence on the monitor.

"Look," I say. "There's our baby's head."

I click the first snap shot of our child and send it out to the printer. While the machine cranks out the black and white rendition of the screen, I wipe away the gel from Bunny's belly.

I pull her yoga pants up and her tee shirt down and finally find the courage to look at her face again.

Her voices trembles. "You said, *our baby.*"

She studies my face and I can't understand what she's looking for. Her question give me a clue, it's certainty.

"You have no doubts?"

None at all and if I was a brave man, now would be the right time to confess what I have done.

"There must have been a tear or something ..."

I put a finger to her lips to hush her. Maybe I can sweep the *accident issue* under the rug.

"How it happened doesn't matter, does it?" Gosh, I'm such a coward. "I'm just happy he's here."

"*He,*" she squeals. "It's a boy?"

"Yeah. A boy unless, of course, that was a piece of umbilical cord I saw between the legs."

Bunny mocks punch me.

"And if I hadn't wanted to know?"

"Then you'd be shit out of luck, my love."

The way she smiles at my term of endearment melts my heart again. I'm bending over to kiss her when a knock on the door stops me.

"I'm sorry, Doctor," the technician says. "But I'll need the room back now. I have two *scheduled* patients waiting."

15

BUNNY

As we ride back to my place, I get lost in the contemplation of my son's profile. Technology is amazing. The baby is still in me, all wrapped up, protected and cozy for a few more months, but I can already see what he'll look like.

Doc drives. He's been very quiet since we got in my car. I break the silence. "You're right, we need to talk."

"It's no longer the first order of business."

"Of course, first thing is to check on Dad," I concede.

"Nope there's something more urgent we need to do." He glances at me and notices my frown. What could be more urgent?

"This has been my longest dry ever..." His tone is so weird I'm not sure if he's joking or not.

"You want to have sex?"

My question makes him grin. "Yeah, don't you?"

"Of course, I do." The words come out before I take the time to think. I catch myself and temper the enthusiasm of my spontaneous answer. "But not before we have a serious discussion."

"So you wanna fight first?"

I roll my eyes at him. "I said discussion, not fight."

He frowns as if I'm not making sense. Thinks it over for a few seconds and asks, with his eyes on the road, "Can I make a suggestion?"

I nod and wonder what he's going to come up with.

"What if we had sex first? Then we could talk. We could even fight if you want."

"Why do you insist I want to argue with you?"

He throws a sideway glance at me, and with a perfect poker face gives me an absurd answer. "'Cause I think make up sex could be fun."

I want to laugh, but instead I bite my lip. He's so adorable, I could instantly wipe his slate clean, but then I would resent it. So no, today I won't give in so easily.

"Oh come on, Bunny, give me at least a smile, that was funny."

"Yeah, when you're around, you're a funny guy." As the words escape from my lips, I realize how much pain I have been smothering the past six months. I didn't want to admit it, even to myself, but his silence hurt so damned much.

Unable to ignore the shift in my mood, Doc gives up his sales pitch for a quickie to quench his thirst. "Okay, we'll talk, if you want, but not in the car."

Contradictory is my middle name for the day.

"Why not, this seems like a perfect place?"

"No, it's not." He shakes his head. "Not at all. 'Cause, you see, when we do talk, I want to hold you and tell you how sorry I am I messed up so badly." I hold my breath. He probably doesn't realize, but we're actually talking. "I don't want to have my eyes on the road, but on you when I promise it will never happen again."

That's the sweetest thing he's ever told me and I badly want to believe him.

"There's no excuse for what I've done. I should have reached out. I should have called you at the bar. At least once... I should have explained."

"Why didn't you?" That's the million dollar question for me.

"I'm not sure."

"You're not getting off this easy," I declare. "You're not a kid who doesn't know why he does things. You're a grown man. A responsible one at that, given your choice of profession. So tell me 'cause..."

He raises a pacifying hand from the steering wheel to stop my torrent of angry words. "All right, all right, gimme a minute."

We're home. He parks in my garage and fumbles with the beeper. The door slides down behind us and he cuts off the engine. I watch him staring at his hands on the steering wheel. His grip is so tense, his knuckles are white.

Time passes and the timer kills the light. Still neither of us makes a move to get out of the car.

"First, I didn't call because I was a dick head."

That's for sure, but not really helpful.

"I missed you so much, calling you was not gonna cut it. It was gonna be like putting salt on a gaping wound. So I decided to wait a bit." He takes a deep breath and in the semidarkness of the garage, I see his hands moving. "Did you ever have to do something so painful that you decided to postpone it?"

My answer is an absolute no. When I have something unpleasant to do, I do it right away to get it over with. No point in having something you dread hanging over your head for days or even hours. But I'm guessing he's not built the same.

"And then the longer you wait the more difficult it gets..." he shifts and reaches out for my hand. "It took me two months to get my head out of my ass. When I did, I swapped hours and rode back to you but you were gone ..."

"That was Labor Day weekend," I whisper putting the dots together.

"How do you know?"

"I left a letter for you with Sam."

"I never got it." He squeezes my hand a little tighter.

"Yeah, he told me. He was out of town that night and no one else knew about it."

We both sigh at the same time and chuckle.

He bends over and brushes my lips with his. His kiss is chaste and pure and ... loving?

"But then Prince asked us to join the Defiance chapter," he says. "Florida was tempting, but what sealed the deal was that he told me you were back in Point Lookout."

He bends over again, and this time, it's a real kiss. One of those that melts my heart. It's not chaste; it speaks of desire.

Doc pulls away, and resting his forehead against mine asks, "Can I safely assume we're done with the talking now?"

I nod bumping our noses together and giggle. Six months of tension have magically evaporated and I'm feeling giddy.

"Can we have sex now?"

"Right this instant?"

The man is incorrigible.

Before I even get a chance to explain that I'm six month pregnant and there's no way we're doing this in the car, Birdy saves me the trouble.

She opens the connecting door and switches on the light. My sister always had a great sense of timing.

Unaware that she could possibly have interrupted something or killed a magic moment, she looks at the washing machine and then at us. She says, "Oh, there you are. What are you doing in the dark? And how come there's not a clean towel in the house?"

16

DOC

"Alone at last," Bunny says as I close the door on the last departing visitor. Between most of the members of the Ryan family tribe and the Tornadoes who rode over to help Brains get home, we haven't had a second to ourselves.

Bunny gets up from her rocking chair and contemplates the mess. Paper plates and plastic cups, half empty food containers and beer cans. Birdy did offer to stay and help clean up, but I declined. All of this can wait until tomorrow.

My dislike for clutter is smothered by my craving for Bunny. I need to touch her, feel her, taste her again. I'm done waiting.

"Is my lady ready for bed?"

She laughs. "You do have a one track mind."

With a mock offended expression on my face, I protest. "I don't remember you ever complaining about it."

Following her to the larger bedroom after making sure all doors are locked, I notice there's something I will need to thank Bunny's sisters for the next time I see them. They made the bed with clean sheets.

Bunny opens the bed and sits. Her shoes fly to the other side of the room and she yawns. "I'm so tired I could fall asleep this instant, fully clothed."

"Ain't gonna happen," I say.

"You're absolutely right. I need to brush my teeth first." The way Bunny smiles at me, I know she's perfectly aware that my main concern was not with her dental hygiene. "Oh, and I have a spare toothbrush for you," she adds as she enters the bathroom.

I undress and follow her into her tiny bathroom. Standing behind her, I look at her face in the mirror while she wipes a bit of toothpaste foam from the corner of her mouth.

"There's something really wrong here."

"Yeah, I know," she says. "I've turned into a blimp." She shrugs sadly, and I wish for the words to tell her how magnificent and desirable she is. But then I realize actions speak louder than words, so instead of shushing her, I press my erection against her back. She feels it and the sides of her lips twitch.

"Nah, what's wrong is that I'm the only one naked and I was looking forward to taking you with me in the shower."

"Oh, you want me to scratch your back?"

"For starters." I turn her around and pull her shirt over her head. "And then I'll inventory my favorite toys." I cup her breasts with my hands. "Rumor has it, I'm gonna have to share them soon."

She laughs and shakes her head. "It will be only a short while. The hotel is not that generous for maternity leave."

Making a mental note to revisit this issue later, I push her yoga pants and her panties down and unhook her bra and let it drop with the rest of her clothes on the floor.

Tentatively she takes my face in her hands and looks into my eyes as if trying to read my thoughts. Too bad it's not possible. I'm not sure who did a number on her head about the way she looks, but if she could see herself the way I do, I'm sure all her insecurities would wash away.

I turn the shower on, adjust the water temperature, and pull her with me under the stream. She closes her eyes and lets the droplets fall on her face. I love the way she looks when she abandons herself to simple sensations like that. One of the most adorable things about her is the precious childlike quality about the way she looks at life and seizes every instant of happiness.

Armed with liquid soap, I complete a full exploration of her body. I savor her sighs and purring noises when I massage her back, but then my favoring some parts over other has her giggling. I raise an inquiring eyebrow. Laughter was not was I was aiming for.

"I think the girls have never been that thoroughly cleaned before."

Okay, fair enough. I may have lingered a while on two of my favorite bits. I take more soap and visit the swell of her belly.

God, I have a child in there. The most precious gift of life. Bunny has stolen my soul and my heart. She's my goddess. As this reality hits, I kneel at her feet. There is no better way to worship her than to put my lips to the stretched skin and then reach below.

The purring sounds start again and I know I got her right on the edge of ecstasy when she leans against the tiled wall and grabs a fistful of my hair.

"Oh, Doc!" Her breathless call washes away the shreds of my restraint. I stand and realize what I had in mind won't work. There's a belly in the way.

Reading my frustration in my eyes, Bunny shuts the water down and pulls the new shower curtain open. Holding my hand, she steps out of the shower and leans forward against the wash basin cabinet. Oh! That's perfect.

I press against her and as she spreads her legs, I find my way to heaven. Holding on to her hips, I stare at the foggy mirror regretting not seeing her face. I always loved to watch her surrender as I pounded into her.

Not soon enough, she moans again and it takes all my self-control not to give in. The sounds escaping from her crescendo until she shudders and draws me with her into our own magnificent slice of heaven.

I grab her robe and wrap it around her before I lead her to bed.

"Hold me," she asks as she pulls the light quilt over us.

I mold my front to her back and embrace her.

This is how I want to fall asleep every night for the rest of my life.

"Oh, that's so sweet," she purrs.

Did I say that out loud? She turns to face me. Her lids are heavy, but she's fighting to stay awake. "But what I need to know is if you said that to the dark beauty who was on your bed when I went looking for you?"

"You came to the Knight's compound?"

She yawns. "Even left you a note on your bedside table."

"Fuck you, Raven," I growl. The next time I see her, I'm gonna tear the little monster a new one.

She snuggles against me and already half asleep whispers, "No, you won't. If you haven't already, then you missed your chance. Now, you're all mine, and I won't share."

I caress her cheek and marvel at the warmth I feel. No matter what happens next, I know how happiness tastes.

I hope you've enjoyed Doc and Bunny's story.

Did you know that if you only leave a star rating on your device, I will never know if you liked the story or not?

The only way I can learn what my readers liked is if I see it reviewed. It only takes two words to make an author's day or inspire us in the middle of the night when we can't sleep searching for a new twist in our next novel.

I am most grateful to those who take a minute to post a positive thought that will encourage others to pick up a copy.

I hope you've enjoyed Bunny and Doc's story.

It's time to catch up with Lisa and Ice in Tornado Warning.

If you turn the page you can "peek a book."

17

BRIAN - FRIDAY

"**F**uck me! Is that a hearse?" Waxer asks to no one in particular.

The entire crew turns to stare at the vehicle making its way into the parking lot.

And yep, it is a damned hearse driving along with the Category 5 Knights crew.

Their team is led by Chaser, their Prez, and Piston, their VP. For a second, I think they left Prince at home, but no, their Sergeant at Arms is closing the convoy. Thor, Dragon, and Peanut ride by the sinister black monster.

"What the fuck!" says Sledge.

Lobster turns a deeper shade of crimson than usual and crosses himself.

The Knights gather next to us in the deserted parking lot of the abandoned gas station and kill their engines.

The door of the black monster opens and I laugh when I see Doc stepping out.

"That kind of car can't be good for business!" I tell him.

He jokes back, "Look at the positive side. If you die in my care, I can take you straight to the cemetery."

"Fair enough," Earplugs says, who has a dark sense of humor.

He and I walk closer to the car. The windows are tinted. We can't see a thing inside.

"Secondhand, it was way cheaper than an ambulance," Chaser explains, "and it works just as well."

"It just needed a bit of customization," Piston adds. "Peanut took care of it."

The Knight prospect beams with pride. I knew their idiot was a bit of a savant when it came to bikes but I guess he's also talented for other stuff. Maybe that's why they brought him along today.

He and Doc are a surprise addition to their team but a welcome one.

"He can only treat one person at a time," Peanut explains, "but he can move more with his three bunks."

Doc smiles at Peanut. "It's not real comfy but it works."

"Great job," I tell the prospect.

The sole presence of Peanut on their team says a lot about Chaser. He's a good man and so is Piston.

As far as I'm concerned, the jury's still out about Prince. Maybe if he wasn't banging my sister, I'd be less suspicious ... or maybe not. There's too many things I don't know about him to let my guard down yet.

"I don't want this thing coming with us," Lobster mumbles while I return to my ride.

I sort of understand where he's coming from. None of us want to be reminded of our own mortality but I like the fact that if something goes wrong, we'll have a doctor handy. One who conveniently forgets to report bullet wounds.

Ignoring Lobster's protest, I kick my bike to life and say, "Let's get this over with."

One by one, we return to the main road, and a couple miles farther south, turn inland until we reach a large clearing. That's where we park. Since we mean this to be a surprise attack, we don't want to announce our arrival with the roar of a dozen Harleys.

It takes a few maneuvers for Doc to turn his hearse around, and when he finally has it facing the dirt road we arrived on, he opens the back door and takes out a couple bags and carries them to the passenger seat.

Lobster leans towards Waxer and says, "I swear he's gonna jinx us!"

"It never hurts to be prepared," Sledge snaps back.

He should know, he's a master chess player. The only one who gives him a run for his money is Whizz and my guy's a fucking genius.

I look around searching for Prince and find him a few feet away staring at me. He nods and I nod back. Last time I was here with him, he had to carry me back 'cause I couldn't see shit.

No more nighttime goggles. This time we're entering at dusk. We may be more visible, but there's more of us and safety in numbers.

Also, we've been watching the place for weeks now and have figured out their routine: school buses are brought here on Friday afternoon after the last kid has been dropped off. The drugs are loaded underneath the buses by a team of three and early Saturday morning they are driven back to their usual parking lots where they remain until Monday morning when they go their different routes to pick up and deliver kids to the schools. What happens to the drugs after that we still have to figure out.

Everest wanted to let drug sniffing dogs loose in the parking facility, but the district attorney's office nixed it as Everest wouldn't reveal his sources. In all likelihood, the judge would have refused a warrant for lack of probable cause.

We can't wait for him to figure out this shit anymore. The official route is so slow that I doubt they can get their act together before the end of the school year in a few months. So yeah, we're going now. There's no way we're gonna wait until the new school year starts in August to put a plug on this.

Also, as Sledge pointed out, if we hit now, chances are we're gonna hurt them bad 'cause they're likely stocking up to make do during the spring break when all the crazies come around.

It makes sense. It could be a seasonal business. After all, the Knights double their inventory of meds for the first quarter of the year. Gotta keep those snow birds healthy so they'll return next winter.

Our small troop slowly walks through the bushes until we reach the weak part of the fence. We pull a few planks out, and one by one, enter the property.

Now that's strange: the place should be packed with half a dozen school buses and the cars of the men who get the stuff ready.

Chase crouches next to me and says, "This don't feel right. It's too silent."

I agree.

"You think we screwed up?" I ask.

"How so?"

"Maybe we waited too long and they rotate delivery methods? I know we do."

Chaser doesn't answer. He turns to Piston who's now crouching on his left.

Piston shrugs and says, "There's only one way to find out."

"You mean storming in?" Chaser asks.

"Yeah, and if there's no one, we'll just destroy their facility," Piston suggests.

"I'm not so sure about that," I answer. "If we tear down the place, they'll just rebuild a new one like they did last time, and we'll have to search for it. At least we know where this one is."

"Why don't we go in and look," Chaser suggests. "We'll see what we find and figure out what to do then."

"Fine with me," I answer. "Let's stick to our original plan."

Our group divides into three teams.

Team Alpha will raid the smaller building. Team Bravo gets the front entrance of the main building while Team Charlie moves in from the back.

We move in like pros. Slow and silent.

Piston, Dragon, Sledge, and I reach our position first and wait for the others to get in place.

From where we stand, we can't see Team Charlie but Team Alpha can and they will signal as soon as Prince, Thor, and Earplugs are in position.

It takes another minute before Waxer, Lobster, Chaser, and Peanut, their last-second addition, are in place.

Chaser raises his hand and starts the countdown.

Next to me, Piston whispers, "I don't like it. It's too quiet."

And just when I think to myself some people should think twice before saying what they wish for, all hell breaks loose.

ALSO BY OLIVIA - BIKERS

The Iron Tornadoes MC Romance Series

Stone Cold - Available in Audio book

Cold Burn - Available in Audio book

Cold Fusion - Available in Audio book

Hot Pursuit

Hot Mess

White Hot

Bumpy Ride

Tornado Warning

Storm Advisory

Hurricane Watch

The Iron Tornadoes MC Romance Next Generation

The Player

The Winner

To be continued

SeriesBundles of the series

Cold (Books 1 to 3) - Available in Audio book

Hot (Books 4 to 6)

Storm (Books 8 to 10)

The Category 5 Knights MC Romance Series

Chaser

Saving Belle

OTHER BOOKS BY OLIVIA

Play with The Curve Masters

As He Bids

Lost and Found

Found and Kept

Kept and Shared

Keeping Tab

STAND ALONE BOOKS

Artistic License (related to the Curve Masters)

Jade

Learning Curves

Ripped (related to the Iron Tornadoes)

Flirting with Disaster with Ava Catori

Flirting with Deception with Ava Catori

Flirting with Danger with Ava Catori

Flirting with Curves (Bundle) with Ava Catori

ABOUT THE AUTHOR

Olivia Rigal is a six-time USA Today bestselling hybrid author of romantic suspense who joined the Indie publishing movement in 2013.

A native New Yorker who has lives for decades in France, Olivia brings a rich personal background to her stories.

In prior lives, she worked in a Paris recording studio, at the Clignancourt Flea Market, as an admin at a world famous auction house in Manhattan, groomed pets and practiced law as licensed attorney in New York and Paris.

These experiences come together in Olivia's novels. While most of the stories she tells are stand alone, beloved characters weave in and out, welcoming readers again and again.

To find out about her latest release, join her
https://oliviarigal.com/vip-group/

When she's not writing, she loves to hang out and chat with readers, you can find her on line.

On Facebook
www.facebook.com/AuthorOliviaRigal
On Instagram
instagram.com/oliviarigal

CONTENTS